CW00858968

Marvin and The Melody Mice

for my friend
Clare

Brenda May Williams

Illustrated by Raymond Williams

Edited by Alec Hawkes

Publishing assistance by Elizabeth Mills

Written by Brenda May Williams and illustrated by Raymond Williams with love for May and Ann.

Hello boys and girls, how would you like to hear a story about Marvin and his Melody Mice? Gather round and I shall begin. Marvin is a very unusual mouse indeed because he is blue and everyone knows that mice are not supposed to be blue.

All of his friends love him and he's also a very talented musician, he plays the trumpet in a band of musical mice called The Melody Mice. Marvin also has a special party trick which involves putting liquid soap inside his trumpet and when he plays, big soapy bubbles come out of the end of it.

Marvin's
Trumpet

The other mice think that Marvin's party trick is odd, but because they love him they let him do it anyway and just put it down to him being the only blue mouse they had ever known. They don't think it's funny though and every time bubbles come out of Marvin's trumpet, they tell him off.

Marvin loves playing in the band and as soon as he plays his trumpet, the audience cheer and clap along. So you see, even though the other members think it's a little odd, the people who come to listen to them play love it. After all, Marvin is blue and bubbles come out of his trumpet, so who could blame them? He is the only blue mouse they have ever seen and blowing bubbles from his trumpet makes him very happy indeed.

Marvin and the Melody Mice

The Bandstand

One day after band practice, Mr Melody, who is the band conductor of the Melody Mice, gathered Marvin and the gang around and announced that he had some very important and exciting news to tell them. So, he cleared his throat and said in a strong voice: 'Melody Mice, I have some exciting news to tell you.'

Tish the Drummer was very interested in this news and couldn't contain her excitement, so she cried out in a loud squeak: 'Oh, please Mr Melody, tell us what it is!' Mr Melody cleared his throat again to begin his announcement in full and as he did so, Marvin squeaked: 'drum roll please.' Tish instantly jumped into action and banged loudly on her drums. She was a very happy little mouse and everyone loved her dearly because she was always bubbly and she cheered them up.

Tish's
Drums

Mr Melody thanked her and said: 'We have been invited to play our music at Gino's Italian Café, if it all goes well, we may be asked to do a regular spot there.' The little band of musical mice was absolutely delighted because they liked Gino's and they knew that his café was the best for miles around.

Oscar, the violin player, was worried about Marvin though; he didn't want to upset anyone because he loved his band mates, but he thought it was important to point out Marvin's unusual trick with the bubbles. So, he plucked up some courage and said: 'what about Marvin? He does that silly thing with the bubbles and he will ruin it for us.'

Oscar's
Violin

Mr Melody was already thinking about this himself and said: 'Marvin, I want you to stop this nonsense with the bubbles for the time being, because this is a very serious audition, can you do that?'

Marvin was annoyed because he liked blowing bubbles, but if there was one thing that he liked better it was Gino's Spaghetti sauce, and he knew there would be lots of that at Gino's place, so he replied: 'Yes, you can count on me Mr Melody.'

Mr Melody promptly nodded and said: 'I hope so. Now, off you all go home and practice playing your instruments, but be sure to arrive on time at the bandstand next week. I'd like you to be polished, ready for the audition of your lives and make me proud of you all.'

So, full of confidence that Mr Melody had belief in them to do the very best they could, off they all went in the direction of home, chattering wildly to each other about how exciting it was going to be.

Jarvis the saxophone player said: 'as long as Marvin behaves himself and doesn't blow bubbles, we shall be brilliant! Everyone agreed and one by one they reached their houses and said goodbye. They all arranged to practice their instruments for the audition, and agreed they would see each other the following week at the park.

Jarvis's
Saxophone

Tish's house was next door to Marvin's, and as she reached her door she said: 'don't you worry Marvin, as long as you don't blow those silly bubbles from your trumpet, I am sure Gino will just love our performance. He may even give us some of his famous spaghetti sauce. See you next week.'

Marvin said goodbye, and made his way home with a heavy heart; he loved blowing bubbles, and he thought that the show wouldn't be the same without them. He wanted to please his friends though, and he put it out of his mind. He decided to just concentrate on practising his musical skills for the audition, and hoped it would be a success.

On the day of the audition at Gino's Place, the Melody Mice had been instructed to meet Mr Melody at the bandstand in the park. They had also been told to wash their hands and faces, and to make sure that their uniforms were clean and neat. So every mouse knew they had to make the very best effort to look and sound their best.

Marvin was excited when he woke up that morning and he had butterflies in his tummy; his Mum had made him breakfast, but he was too excited to eat it and she was cross. She could never be cross with Marvin for too long though so, she said: 'You have a big day ahead of you Marvin and breakfast is the most important meal of the day; you are not going anywhere until you've eaten it!'

Marvin's
Mum

Marvin knew she was right of course, so he quickly ate the toast with blueberry jam that his mum had made for him. When he'd finished his breakfast, he cleaned his teeth and looked in the mirror to make sure his hands and face were clean. When he was sure all was well, he put his uniform on, and happily said: 'Bye Mum, wish me luck.'

His Mum chuckled, kissed him on the head and said: 'Good luck Marvin and most of all, have fun.' He cheerfully skipped out of the door, collecting his lovely, shiny trumpet on the way and made his way to Tish's house so they could both go to the park together.

He knocked on Tish's door and she answered it with a big smile on her face; she was a lovely little mouse and Marvin really liked her.

He commented on how nice she looked in her clean uniform, and she returned the compliment , saying: 'Oh, thank you Marvin, my Mum was up all night making sure it was just right, you look great too.' Marvin thanked her and they both said goodbye to her Mum. Tish's Mum wished them luck as they left, and they both happily skipped to the park.

Tish's
Mum

Tish suddenly stopped and said: 'I hope you haven't got any liquid soap with you because you know it's an important audition.' Marvin assured her that he didn't, and the two mice continued on their way in the direction of the park, where all of the other mice would be waiting. When they arrived they could see the other band members excitedly chattering away to each other about what a wonderful day they would have together, and it must be said that each mouse looked spotless and well-polished.

Mr Melody arrived shortly after them and, when he saw them, his heart was bursting with pride. He just couldn't have been any happier, because every single mouse looked amazing in their uniforms ,and he felt very proud of his little band. He said: 'Thank you for coming and if we don't get this spot at Gino's place every week after this, I will eat my hat!'

Marvin was happy and said: 'You won't have to eat your hat Mr Melody, we will make you very proud of us and I'm not going to blow bubbles today.'

Mr Melody's
hat

Mr Melody was pleased. He walked to his truck, which was very big, and said: 'Jump in the back Melody Mice, we are off to impress Gino.' The truck was very comfortable in the back and there was plenty of room, so they took the opportunity for one last practice.

Marvin played the trumpet very loudly, but beautifully; he was pleased because everyone was in perfect harmony. He still couldn't help thinking that there was something missing, and then it hit him! There were no bubbles coming out of his trumpet.

Tish had noticed a sad look on his face, and said: 'Cheer up Marvin, I know you like the bubbles, but we are professionals, and that means no bubbles, just music.' Marvin was sad, but of course he knew that she was right, and replied: 'I know Tish, I will do my very best today, don't worry.'

Gino's place wasn't very far away, and they were there in no time at all. Mr Melody pulled the truck up outside the café, he looked over his shoulder and said: 'Okay gang, we are here, now it's time for us to focus.'

Every mouse said in harmony: 'We will,' and with that he got out of the truck and helped The Melody Mice into the Café to set up their instruments.

Gino was a round little man with rosy cheeks and a big bushy moustache; he was very pleased to see them and said: 'Welcome my friends, come inside. I have made some snacks, help yourself and just let me know when you are ready to start.'

Gino

Everyone tucked into the delicious snacks, especially Marvin and as he did so he thought to himself: *'I hope Gino likes our performance, I don't think Mr Melody will like eating his own hat, especially as these snacks are so delicious',* and gave a little chuckle. But of course the snack time had to come to an end, and it was now time to get down to the serious business of playing for Gino.

Mr Melody announced with pride: 'Melody Mice, let's play our music for these fine people.' Every mouse excitedly took their positions, got themselves ready and waited for Mr Melody to tap his baton on his music stand, which would be the signal that the fun was about to begin. He looked over to them all and said: 'Good luck, I am very proud of you all.' And with that he tapped the baton and said: 'Play.' The Melody Mice excitedly began to play.

Tish played sweetly on the drums, Oscar's violin solo could melt your heart, Jarvis was in perfect tune on his saxophone and Marvin played the Trumpet beautifully. The music that they made together really was the sweetest sound that anyone would hear. Mr Melody was thrilled and very proud when he heard them play. He also had a big smile on his face because he knew that they were all in great tune.

All of a sudden Mr Melody glanced over his shoulder to see what Gino was doing; he became concerned because Gino was just sat at a table watching and listening to the music, but his face was glum. Mr Melody began to worry because he thought Gino didn't seem to be enjoying the music, and this made him sad because his little band had practiced very hard for this.

Poor Mr Melody did not know what to do, so he did the only thing he could and that was to encourage everyone. He waved his baton in the air and invited the café staff to clap their hands in time to the music, but everyone just stood around in silence.

When the music finished, not one single person in the restaurant clapped. Mr Melody was very confused and he said: 'Gino, my mice have played their little hearts out, didn't you enjoy it?'

Gino was a kind man and didn't want to upset Mr Melody, so he simply said: 'It was nice, but there just seemed to be something missing. I am sorry, but I don't think I can let you play at my café, Mr Melody.'

Gino was sad; he shook his head and said to the mice: 'The last time I heard you play, Marvin blew beautiful big bubbles from the end of his trumpet, and I loved it. I didn't see you do that this time Marvin.'

Marvin jumped up and said: 'Gino, if you want bubbles, I am going to blow the biggest bubbles you have ever seen; fetch me some liquid soap from the kitchen.'

Mr Melody was concerned, and was just about to protest, but someone had already gone to the kitchen to fetch the soap. So he figured he'd just see what would happen.

Liquid soap

When the waitress returned from the kitchen with the soap, Marvin instantly put it into his trumpet and when he was satisfied that there was enough, he gathered the mice around and said: 'Come on Melody Mice, let's show Gino what we are made of. Mr Melody, can you please count us in?' Mr Melody replied: 'Of course Marvin, I will be delighted to.'

He walked back over to the music stand, took a deep breath and prepared to count The Melody Mice in, and this time he just knew that his mice would show Gino that they were the best bubble-blowing band of musical mice for miles around. Just before the music began, he said to Marvin: 'I am sorry Marvin, you were right all along. I am very proud of you all.' With that, he tapped the baton again and the music began. Only this time, when Marvin blew his trumpet, the biggest bubbles anyone had ever seen came out of the end of it.

Gino was thrilled and so was everyone else in the café. They were so thrilled, in fact, that they all sang along, danced in time to the music, and clapped their hands.

When the music stopped, everyone had happy smiles on their faces, and they all cried out for more. They actually wanted the mice to continue playing because they were having such fun. So that's what they did; they played and played until they got tired. The Melody Mice just knew that everyone had enjoyed their performance.

After the second performance, Gino took Mr Melody aside and said: 'Marvin and The Melody Mice will be the star attraction in my café, Mr Melody, I am so happy. Can you play here every Saturday morning?'

Well, as you can imagine, Mr Melody was thrilled and accepted his kind offer. He was delighted that his little mice had entertained everyone so well, but more importantly he was happy they had passed this audition.

He was also very relieved that he didn't need to eat his own hat, and with that he turned to Marvin and said: 'Marvin, I am so sorry that I told you not to blow bubbles.' Marvin replied: 'Don't worry Mr Melody, everything worked out just fine in the end.'

Everyone agreed that it had indeed all worked out just fine in the end and, as Marvin and the rest of the mice loved Mr Melody, they didn't want him to ever be upset. They all gathered around and patted him on the back, because they were just as pleased as he was. Tish said: 'Oh, Mr Melody, you really are the best band leader any band of musical mice could have.'

This cheered him up no end, so he thanked them all and told them how proud he was of them.

It was then that Gino asked them all if they would like more snacks; so of course every mouse said: 'Yes please,' at the same time ,and they instantly gathered around the beautiful, brightly coloured table and tucked into some of Gino's famous spaghetti sauce.

Gino's
spaghetti sauce

When they had finished their delicious meal, every Melody Mouse had full tummies, including Mr Melody, who was pleased that the food most certainly did taste better than he thought his hat would have. Even though it was a very nice hat indeed, he still didn't want to eat it.

With that, Gino thanked everyone and politely asked them to be at his café at ten o'clock sharp the next week for the debut performance. Every mouse smiled from ear to ear. They really were going to be the talk of the town and Marvin's bubbles were certain to bring crowds of people into the café, they were sure of it.

So, with goodbyes and thank yous said, they set off home to tell their parents the wonderful news that they were now a band of mice who were going to be the star attraction at Gino's Italian Café every Saturday morning.

As you'll all imagine, the mice were very excitable on the trip home in the truck, because everyone was so happy in the knowledge that not only would they be playing at Gino's Café every week, but they would also be very spoilt, and very well fed by Gino. They all knew they were loved by everyone, and Mr Melody's Musical Mice were going to be very famous indeed.

Can you colour

Tish here

?

Well, boys and girls, I hope you enjoyed my little book. You can now see Marvin and the Melody Mice playing their wonderful music at Gino's Italian Café every Saturday morning.

They really do hope that you will pop in to see them one day and try Gino's famous spaghetti sauce; it's the very best spaghetti sauce for miles around. All you have to do is ask Marvin, he loves it, but most of all you will be amazed at those big, soapy bubbles that Marvin blows from the end of his trumpet.

Goodnight, sleep tight.

Love from Brenda May xx

21720756R00026

Printed in Great Britain
by Amazon